Our First Pony

By MARGUERITE HENRY
Illustrated by Rich Rudish

 RAND M^cNALLY & COMPANY • Chicago • New York • San Francisco

Copyright © 1984 by Rand McNally & Company.   All rights reserved.
Printed in the United States of America by Rand McNally & Company.

LIBRARY OF CONGRESS CATALOG CARD NUMBER: 84-13409

Most of this story happened in a barn. Milk cows used to live in it. Then they were sold, and the building looked forlorn until. . . well that's our story, and it happened like this.

NO ONE ever said that Joseph and Justin were alike as two peas in a pod, even though they were twins. Joseph had hair the color of ripe wheat. Justin's was shiny dark.

But more distinct, they lived in opposite worlds. Joseph loved land and sky and grass, and animals – the twin goats, Abraham and Isaac; and the three dogs, Trimmer, Andy and Long John; and the small creatures scrabbling in the hayloft, especially Pauline, a talkative cat who furnished all the kittens.

Justin was fond of them too, but his hobbies were reading and music. He played the piccolo in the school band. Different as the two boys seemed, yet they were completely in tune.

On this early Saturday morning in the beginning of April, Justin was practicing on his piccolo when Joseph burst into their bedroom and tossed the classified section of the *Morning Bugle* on the music stand, atop the sheet music. Justin brushed the newspaper to the floor. He was only slightly peeved. He blew an ear-piercing blast on his piccolo and laid the instrument on the music stand. "Can't you see I'm busy?"

"Well, I'm bus*ier*."

"Doing what?"

"Policing the goats or else they eat the dogs' food and lap up Pauline's milk, and she's got five kittens to nurse."

"So why the newspaper?"

"I haven't time to read the ads. Besides," he said, "you read quicker."

"What do you want to buy or sell?"

"A pony."

"Well since you haven't got one to sell, you must want to buy one. Why?"

"First off, to help me deliver my papers. Second off, because nobody at school likes me. Not my teacher or the kids."

"Well, *I* like you."

"I know you do, but because we're twins that's like me liking me! But a pony'd like me because I'd feed and water him. He'd belong to me and we could tell each other secrets. Maybe then the kids at school would like me. I could give 'em free rides."

"Or maybe charge 5¢?" Justin suggested.

"Maybe. But most of all, I'd like to be a winner in the Pet and Pony Show."

"You could enter the goats." Justin burst into laughter at the thought. "You could be a trick circus clown. . . riding with one leg on Abraham, one on Isaac."

Even Joseph had to laugh. "Remember last year's show? They were just kids then, and they broke free and played leap frog all the way around the ring." The boys laughed so hilariously that John and Mary, both in their teens, left the breakfast table and bounded up the stairs.

"Sh. . . sh." Joey pinched his lips shut and nodded at Justin to do the same.

"What do you want me to do?" Justin whispered.

"You read all the ads and if you find a good one, bust out to the barn and tell me."

Mary and John poked their heads in the doorway, then shrugged and left. The twins, they concluded, could laugh over anything or nothing.

"Jus–tin! Your oatmeal's getting cold." Mom Franklin's summons had a no-nonsense ring. She roughed up Justin's hair, as he showed up with the *Morning Bugle* under his arm.

"I swear," she said, smiling, "you're getting more like your father every day, always with your nose in a book or paper." She placed a steaming bowl of oatmeal in front of him.

Justin gulped his cereal, reading, running his finger down the columns until he pounced on two exciting prospects.

He put his bowl in the sink and hurried out to the barn where

Joseph was carrying on a four-way conversation with Pauline mrr-aow-ing from the loft, with the goats ba-aa-ing in chorus, and with Andy crunching on a piece of wood. At the sight of Justin, Joey shooed the animals outdoors.

"Now read to me, little bro," he said. "You make everything sound good."

Flattered, Justin opened to the earmarked page. "Here's one sounds great!" With the basso pitch of a barker at the State Fair he began: "'For sale. Welsh pony mare, daughter of champion McDougal's Folly. Owner moving. Sacrifice at $450...'"

"Whoa!" Joey interrupted. "Stop right there!"

"No, Joey. Listen: 'Real leather halter. Summer and winter blankets included...'"

"I can't afford $450. I could only make a down payment of $68.50. Nobody's going to fall for that."

Unperturbed, Justin had saved the best for the last: "Would you believe this one, big bro? (There was only five minutes difference in their ages, but Justin liked the thought that he had a big brother to fend for him.) 'Pinto Shetland. Tobiano color pattern. 10 years old. 11.2 hands. 100% sound. Nice manners. Good trail pony. Free to exceptional family. Contact R. Wolter. Oak Creek Farm. 553-3325.'"

Joey ran out of the barn, turned three cartwheels and shouted to the world. "She's just as old as me!"

"And me!" Justin yelled. "But what about 11.2 hands? And what does Tobiano mean?" Joseph took a running leap on Abraham's back. "Who cares?" he whooped. "She's free! And we're an ex-cep-tion-al family."

The Oak Creek Farm of R. Wolter seemed more park than farm. A tree-lined lane ended in a circle before a turreted house overlooking a lake. Joey and Justin bypassed the house and beelined for the

open barn, almost bumping into a large man coming out. Except for his white hair and beard being close cropped, he could have played Santa Claus, Joey thought. "Are you Mr. Wolter?" he asked.

"That I am, and whom do I have the honor of addressing?"

Joey wanted to laugh out, for even Mr. Wolter's voice boomed as deep as any Santa Claus's.

"I'm Joey, and this is my twin, Justin. John and Mary and our Mom are right behind us. We're here to see about the pony."

R. Wolter waited politely for the rest of the clan, then made everyone feel welcome. "It 'pears to me," he said, "that Joey and Justin have brought their advisers along." He beckoned everyone to follow him into the stable. It really wasn't much bigger than the

Franklins' barn at home; but it smelled of hay instead of goats, and there were two muscly quarter horses in side-by-side stalls, their coats polished to a gloss. An elderly Dalmatian came out of a straw nest, growling deep in his throat, his tail wagging at the same time.

"Polka Dot is slightly deaf," R. Wolter said, "but he pretends he's fierce. Actually he loves people, just like our Shetland. Now come along and meet my daughter's pride and joy."

In single file the five Franklins followed down a corridor lined with bales of straw and out into a sun-filled pasture where a pinto pony looked up from a flake of hay with wisps of it sticking out between her lips. At sound of Mr. Wolter's voice she let the hay fall and spoke to him in high whinnies.

Joey and Justin stood transfixed. The pony's body-coat was blacker than fresh-poured tar, while her mane and tail were stark white. She had splashy white markings, too, which made her different from any pony they'd ever seen. Barely above a whisper Joey asked, "What's her name?"

"Her *registered* name is Miniature Heirloom."

Joey winced. "Gee. . . do you call her that?"

"Ho no! Of course not. We call her Mini or Midge. She answers to both."

"Hmmm. . ." Joey smiled in relief. "I like that." He pretended he was already her owner, calling her in from pasture. "Mini e-e-e!" he sang out.

The pony flickered an ear in Joey's direction.

"She likes me! She likes me!"

"Wait a minute son, wait a minute. Thirty-five families have already come to see her."

Joey felt a sinking sensation. "You ain't decided?"

R. Wolter took a long time answering. He scruffed his beard, then rubbed Mini behind her ears.

"No-oo-o," he said, "that is, not quite. I plan to visit all thirty-five homes, and yours too to see where my daughter's pet would be happiest. My daughter, by the way, has married and moved far away. She wants to give the pony to the right family."

Suddenly the interview was over. Mr. Wolter shook hands all around. Joey felt a note of hope. "Sir," he said, "you're going to like our barn and our Dad! And Mini's going to like Abraham and Isaac, and the dogs and Pauline, and even our honky goose."

Mr. Wolter threw back his head in a booming laugh which stopped short when he heard a car spitting gravel on the driveway and saw a bunch of children straining out the windows of a camper.

On the way home everyone tried not to think about that camperful of children, especially the strapping boy wearing the red baseball cap. The twins knew him. He was Spike Johnson, the class bully from their school. How would he treat a fine pony like Midge?

For days no word came from R. Wolter, but every free moment was spent in a fever of activity — scraping old cow dung from the hardpacked floor of the barn, replacing it with wheelbarrows full of fresh clean dirt, building a manger, arguing over just how high it should be placed for Midge.

"Don't count on that pony," Mr. Franklin warned. "I've been wanting for a long time to build a good manger for Abraham and Isaac, and now you've done it for me."

But John and Mary and even college student, Peter, Jr., had caught Joey's optimism. They climbed stepladders and swept away cobwebs and old wasps' nests.

At night the twins were so tired they fell asleep before they fell into bed. They dreamed of Mini playing tag with Abraham and Isaac, Mini swimming in the pond with honky goose, Mini chasing the dogs and the dogs chasing her. Yet whenever her name was called out, she came in at a trot.

"Days of waiting are harder than a definite yes or no," Mrs. Franklin said one Sunday morning when the family breakfasted together. "Expectant mothers feel this strongly," she explained. "Will the baby *ever* arrive? Will it be well and whole?" She looked at Joey and Justin in concern. "Your worry is equally hard to bear."

Almost like a stage play, the sound of heavy footsteps and three dogs yapping announced a visitor who turned out to be none other than R. Wolter himself.

"Did you bring Min—" Joey started to say, then he noticed the pickup in the driveway with no van attached.

Mr. Wolter seemed genuinely sorry. "This is just an inspection tour," he said.

"Won't you come into the house for a homemade Danish and a cup of coffee?" Mrs. Franklin asked.

"Thank you, I'd like that, but I've two more stops to make before noon. Suppose the twins introduce me to Mr. Franklin and then take me out to the barn to meet their menagerie."

Joey and Justin were close to tears when the pickup pulled away. "He hardly asked us anything," Justin said. "He didn't even shake hands," Joey said.

The not-knowing made school and homework intolerable. Tempers flared. The twins fought over nothing at all.

"If only he'd said *no* right then," Mary said. "Well, I'm not going to let the suspense get me down. Mini's not a horse anyway," she said. "She's just a pony and you'll soon outgrow her. Then you'll be in Mr. Wolter's shoes trying to find a home for her."

But Joey never gave up. He was the least surprised one morning when his father picked up the phone, and from across the room Joey could hear the booming voice of R. Wolter.

Mr. Franklin, however, didn't know at first who was calling until Joey mouthed the name and began turning somersaults. "Ah, yes! Mr. Wolter! There's a high spirited lad here who would very much like to talk to you."

Joey lost his voice completely, but he really didn't need it. Mr. Wolter did all the talking. "You were right, Joey. I liked your entire family. As for Mini, she'll love being able to run in and out of doors without being boxed in a stall. And think of the fun she'll have with the goats, the dogs and the cat. They'll make delightful stable-mates. See you this afternoon."

Mini arrived at the Franklins' farm in a shiny red van. She trotted down the ramp of the tailgate and into the pasture with complete confidence. Suddenly she spied Abraham and Isaac coming at her, charging, heads lowered to butt her in roughhouse play.

In panic she ran along the fenceline heading for the safety of her van which was barreling down the road, homeward bound. Only the fence rails stopped her. But they didn't stop the goats who leaped up and over and took off for the woods.

After that introduction, even though the goats were dehorned and butted only in fun, Mini regarded them as monsters. If they so much as showed their beards in the barn or ba-aa-aa'd in her direction, she flew out the door running and kicking until she lathered in sweat. Or, if she were rolling contentedly in the pasture and suddenly spied the goats, she high-tailed it to the barn as if two devils with red hot pitch forks were after her.

But one May day when the world was all pink with bloom, Abraham and Isaac tried a new approach. They slow-footed toward her, snuffing and sifting the difference of her smell from theirs.

Snuffing! Ah, this was a process she understood. She snuffed back at them. Then she stood quite still. Her attitude said plainer than any words "Why, you're not so fierce after all!" And this was the beginning of a new friendship. In no time the goats and Mini became inseparable.

As for Joey's popularity, it zoomed. He felt good about himself as a whole, and the kids felt good about him. He quit turning around in class, and hadn't been punished for a long time.

The girls who loved horses now flocked to Franklins' pasture to see what a pedigreed pony with the fancy name of Miniature Heirloom looked like. Their squeals of approval made the twins glow. "She's special," said one. "She's bound to win the Best Pony Class in the Pet and Pony Show next month."

"She may not know it," said snobby Samantha Saunders. "Black-and-white is the designer color this spring."

Jennifer Winquist, whose father was a veterinarian, spoke like a true horsewoman. "Aren't Mini's eyes dark and lustrous," she exclaimed. "That's unusual for a Tobiano. Often they have light-colored eyes. And her markings are wonderful – four white stockings and a white 'blanket' over her thighs." Then she added a bit of advice. "If my Dad were here, he'd say, 'Better go easy on her feed.'"

In late June, Spike Johnson swaggered over to the Franklins'
place on a hot afternoon when Joey and Justin were sloshing Mini
down with cool water. "Hi Fatso!" he said, talking directly to her.
"I knowed ponies was 'sposed to be small, but even soppin' wet
you're broad as you're high."

Joey wanted to throw the wet sponge in Spike's face. "She ain't
either fat!"

"Sometimes small is big," Justin said. "That makes her strong
enough to carry both of us."

"Betcha you can't ride her double."

"Betcha we can!"

Mini was so slippery-sided from her bath that the boys made three attempts before they could stay aboard. Then they traveled a neat course at a spanking pace around the perimeter of the pasture. All the while Spike's guffaws made the boys furious. What in the world could he be laughing at?

"You should see yourselves!" Spike choked between spasms of hilarity. "That cob o' yours is so fat your legs stick out like you're doing the splits."

It was all Joey could do to cut down on Midge's feed when she enjoyed it so much. But Spike's calling her Fatso, plus Jennifer's warning made him divide her portions of sweet feed to last her two days instead of one.

"It hurts," he said to Justin, "to see her when she cleans up every last oat and begs for more."

Justin said, "Couldn't we eat half a candy bar instead of a whole one? That way she wouldn't be fasting all alone."

Joey agreed. "We've got to get her in condition!"

School closed the first week in June, and every family who owned so much as an oversized turtle or a white hamster thought of little else than the Pet and Pony Show. This year, as always, it would be held in Giles's meadow. R. Wolter was to be one of the judges.

"So how can we miss?" The twins asked each other without even saying the words.

"We *could* ride double," Joey offered, crossing his fingers behind his back.

"No. John's asked me to help him fix up his old soap box derby racer; he thinks Abraham and Isaac could pull us in the parade."

"Yeah? That's neat!" Joey said, grinning in relief.

"But I'll still help you train Midge."

Each day, megaphone in hand, Justin pretended he was the announcer. *"Walk Your Ponies Please! Let Them Walk Please! Reverse Your Ponies Please. . ."* Midge soon knew the verbal commands, with or without any signals from Joey.

Not to be left out of the show Mary helped muck out a neighbor's barn, hoping the owner would let her ride his half-Arabian in the costume class. At the last minute he did, and Mrs. Franklin created a costume right out of *Arabian Nights*.

Early on the morning of June 13, Joey practiced his short thank-you sentence for whoever might be presenting him with the blue ribbon, and maybe a trophy too.

The Show began with the grand parade of owners and pets. Kindergartners to teenagers stepped smartly along or dawdled, depending on the whims of their mongrels or purebreds. There were cats wearing dresses and bonnets, jumping in and out of their doll buggies. An anteater, several snakes, an alligator, and an emu topped off the exotics list; but they didn't win a thing. A mongrel named Pickles, wearing false rabbit ears, stole the parade by walking

on his forepaws. Even disappointed kids and their parents cheered the indisputable winner as the most talented pet.

No one expected Abraham and Isaac to win anything except hoots and guffaws, but a special award was given for the goats' magic way-of-going; that is, more leaps and springs upward than forward. Samantha Saunders squeamishly fastened a ribbon to each makeshift bridle while the audience shrieked in laughter when Abraham promptly ate his, slobbering on Samantha's new dress.

To the Franklins' astonishment everyone in the family won a ribbon! Mary, floating around the ring on the Arabian, took a third.

As for Joey, his class for the best all-around pony would be the last of the day, but it was worth the waiting! He was so proud of Mini, Midge that unconsciously he whispered both of her names as the competition began. He knew he had never been happier. His pony seemed to anticipate the commands blaring over the loud speaker: *"Walk Your Ponies! Trot Your Ponies! Slow Canter Your Ponies Please! Remember, The Judges Want Rhythm Not Speed."*

Midge remembered. Joey thought he saw R. Wolter smile, but he wasn't sure. His little Shetland changed from one gait to another as smooth as water flowing downhill. She cantered with rhythm, not speed. She reversed with the grace of a ballet dancer. She performed as if all this routine was old hat to her.

All the while the judges — two men and a large lady in a flowered hat — were making notes on little pieces of paper. Then they whispered in a huddle. At last they waved three entries out of the ring and invited seven to stay. Midge was among the stayers!

"Dismount Your Ponies Please. Remove Your Saddles Please." Joey placed his saddle alongside Midge, and took a sidewise glance at her. She was by far the most sleekly beautiful in the lineup.

The third judge, a little cricket of a man, rocked back and forth on his heels. Importantly he made his decision, barely waiting for the nod from his fellow judges. Two more entries were dismissed.

Now five were left. The moment had come! Silently Joey rehearsed his acceptance speech, but he didn't need it. The blue ribbon, the red, the yellow, the white went to the other ponies. Nothing was left for Midge but a last-place pink ribbon.

For one hurt moment, Joey blinked back his tears, pretending not to care. Then he stroked Midge's neck and trotted her out of the ring, last in line. Slowly, by a back road, he walked Midge home. Her head nudged his shoulder as he stuffed the sissy pink ribbon inside his pocket next to a handkerchief wet with tears.

As evening came on, Joseph's and Justin's sadness turned to anger. What kind of man was R. Wolter anyway — not to convince the judges to vote for Midge?

"Betcha he would've," Joey said, "if his old daughter still owned her!"

Mr. Franklin defended the man. "Boys, that's why they have more than one judge," he said. "Mr. Wolter couldn't swing everybody's vote. He'll give us an answer soon enough and you'll correct whatever needs correcting, and next year maybe you'll own a champ. . ."

He ended the palaver with a glance out the window. A familiar pickup, raising a billow of dust, was turning into the driveway. Two men got out. One was R. Wolter, the other, Jennifer's father, Dr. Winquist. The doctor wore a wide bristly mustache and a smile to match. R. Wolter's face looked older, the twins noticed. Their anger melted when he said, "You boys deserve an explanation."

In the silence that followed, the drip, drip of the kitchen faucet came as loud as hammer strokes. Mrs. Franklin turned up the flame under the coffee pot as the men entered the kitchen. "This time you'll sit down with us?" Mr. Wolter smiled his answer and slid his chair in between the twins.

"No thank you," the doctor said, "while there's still enough daylight I have some examining to do." The boys started to accompany him, but R. Wolter motioned them back.

"Midge's performance this afternoon was spectacular," he said to them, "but it was her conformation. . . 'Barrel is too sprung,' the judges said, 'for her delicate frame.'"

"But we did cut her feed!" Justin wailed.

"That's why I brought Dr. Winquist along to take a look at her. She always was an easy keeper, but maybe there's some glandular disturbance. Winquist will give us his verdict."

"If I remember Midge's habits," Dr. Winquist remarked over his shoulder, "she'll be inside the barn now that the sun's down."

"Goll-eee," the boys gasped at his knowing.

R. Wolter sugared his coffee. "How about you fellows finishing that pudding and then run along to the barn." The pudding disappeared like magic. The screen door banged, and the boys were off.

Quite out of breath they burst in on the doctor, their eyes wide in curiosity. They watched him take a plastic glove out of his pocket then change his mind and put it back. They watched him wind the cord around a twitch, but lay it aside. Carefully and deliberately he walked around Midge, pressing his hand along her belly on both sides, then studying her milk bag. The goats butted in, asking for some hand-pressing too. Pauline on the ladder looked down as much as to say, "I know all about these things."

Dr. Winquist turned to the boys and made his prognosis slowly, precisely. "Miniature Heirloom is due very shortly to foal, and no question about it, there could be more than one inside her!"

Joey let out a whoop loud enough to arouse Abraham and Isaac. Then he and Justin asked the same question. "How come R. Wolter didn't tell us?"

"He didn't know."

"*He didn't know?*" they repeated in chorus.

"He could only guess that while he was away visiting his daughter, a champion Welsh stallion that lives down the road ran away, jumped Midge's fence and came a-calling."

Joey and Justin stared at each other, thunderstruck at the idea of their new responsibilities. But Abraham and Isaac, and Pauline and the dogs made a tumult of harmony as if one or more new occupants in the barn made no difference at all.

The next morning the twins threw their arms around Midge and hugged her with a new awareness. They felt of her sides, imagining they could hear twin heartbeats.

It was very early. Midge's first whicker of welcome rose as usual to higher pitch – anxious for her morning feeding. The change in tone was no different than yesterday's, but the boys read a new meaning. Justin was sure the flutelike blowing through her nostrils was softer, gentler.

Jennifer Winquist showed up just when Joey was pouring Midge's oats. She had a book under her arm, the cover well worn.

"Dad wants to share this book with you," she said. But she held onto it as if it were a beloved possession.

Justin had to tilt his head to read the title. "*The Horseman's Encyclopedia,*" he pronounced, "by Margaret Cabell Self."

Does that book say anything about where colts should be born?"
Joey asked. "In a barn like this, or out in the pasture?"

Jennifer watched Midge grinding her oats. She still held onto
the book. "Yes it does," she answered. "In the wild the mare steals
away from the herd to give birth. But a domesticated mare is better
off in a box stall."

"Hmmm! We'll build a box stall! Does the book tell how?"

Suddenly Jenny was proud to be giving the book away. "Yes,"
she said, "There's a section on stables – it tells how to build anything
as small as a manger or big as a box stall." She placed the book in
Joey's hands. "I got to go now."

Even while thank you's were being called after her Justin was
already checking the table of contents.

Answers came thick and fast as he read aloud while Joey took down the dimensions on the lid of the oatbin:

> Twelve by twelve is the regulation size for the box stall. It may be larger if its occupant is a hunter over sixteen hands. A horse under sixteen hands will get along in a ten by ten. For small ponies eight by eight is ample.

"I vote for 12 x 12," Joey said.

"Me too. 'The side walls,' it says, 'should be two-inch oak.'"

"Whew! That's going to cost a lot."

Justin nodded, went on. "'The grain manger and the water pail should be in opposite corners.'"

Mary came high-stepping into the barn, practicing her baton twirling with a long carrot. She noticed the row of numerals on the oatbin. "Playing Tic Tac Toe? Can I get in the game?"

The twins exchanged glances. "It'll cost you," Joey said.

"How much?"

"Lots! We're building a box stall with two-inch walls!"

"*Two inches!* That's probably thicker than our house." Mary was dividing the carrot between Mini and the goats. "Sure I'll help. I'll give you half my baby-sitting money."

John and Peter wanted to be counted in too. After all, R. Wolter had approved the Franklins as a family, and the responsibility weighed on each member. Both boys had summertime jobs. John ran the vegetable stand at neighbor Pearce's farm, and Peter worked at the local grocery as carry-out boy. Slowly the pot grew until it looked rich enough to build a fine box stall.

In mid-July the contributions were totalled and the Franklins, five strong, set off in high spirits for Handyman's Lumber & Hardware Store. The proprietor was impressed. "I like helping out on family projects," he said. He studied the neat draftsman's drawing which John had made, and smiled.

From that hour in the lumber yard time was crucial. Only two months before school opened. "And Midge's twins could come any time," Joey said, "if it works anything like with Pauline."

On the twenty-fourth of July the actual building began. Never before had Peter, Mary, John, Joseph and Justin worked on the same project side by side.

For six days the clamor and din went on – the sawing and hammering, the yelling over beatup fingers, and whoopees over the slightest progress.

The goats gloried in the racket, leaping in and out of the support posts, not minding at all whoever smacked them on the rump and told them to buzz off. The high whine of the power saw sent Trimmer and Long John howling in pain to their ears, but Andy remained in the thick of things, crunching scraps of lumber in ecstasy. As for Midge, she watched in complacent approval.

And so the hot July days passed. On the twenty-ninth the side walls were solidly in place and work began on the half door, with a reading by Justin from the encyclopedia:

> Box stalls may have dutch doors; that is, divided across the middle. The occupant will enjoy putting his head out and watching what is going on around him.

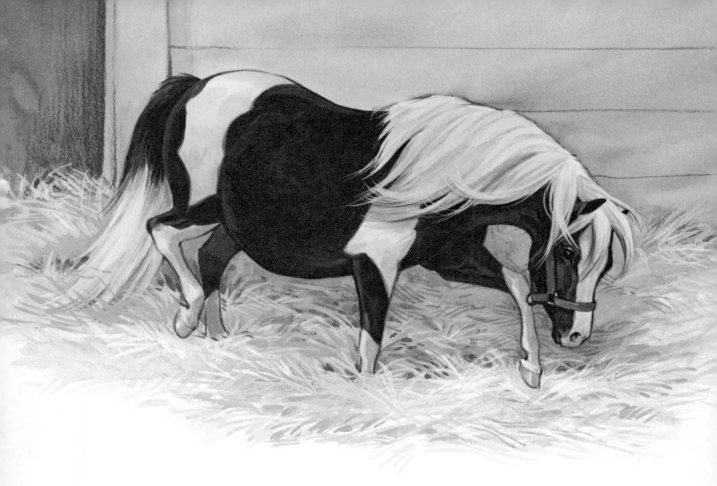

On July 31 the door was finished, the straw laid, the manger filled with hay, the water bucket filled with cool well water, and Midge's stall was ready and waiting. She tiptoed over the tickly straw, going in and out to satisfy her curiosity.

That first day she tolerated occasional visits from Abraham and Isaac, but if they overstayed their welcome she pinned back her ears in silent warning. It was obvious that Miniature Heirloom had taken full possession of her own box stall.

As Midge's foaling time drew near the boys worried. What should they do about her care? What could they do to help?

They sought out Dr. Winquist in his clinic and worked out a happy solution. After school each day they'd swab the doctor's floors and empty his surgical buckets. In return they could have an appointment to ask all the questions they wanted and get instant answers:

"Should we stop riding Midge?"

"On the contrary! She should be exercised every day. But don't exhaust her or let her get overheated."

"Is it all right for her to eat more right now?"

"No! It isn't all right! Extra weight will make her uncomfortable. It might even add to the colts' struggles to be born."

"But can't we give her *any*thing special?"

"Yes! Make sure she's getting enough bonemeal in her diet, and be sure to put on a pony-proof lock on her oatbin."

As time went on the questions became more serious: "What should we do while Midge's twins are being born?"

Dr. Winquist thundered his answer. "Stay away! Leave her alone. Respect her privacy."

"Aw gee, can't we help at all?"

"Well. . . Midge *might* let you clean one foal's nostrils and help to rub its coat dry while she looks after the other foal."

Eventually it was Dr. Winquist asking the questions: "Is Midge's milk bag waxing, getting noticeably fuller, getting hard to the touch, and sensitive?"

"Is it ever! Even when we're brushing her she lays her ears back if we get anywhere close."

"Does she sleep lying down now, with her feet folded underneath her?"

"Yeah, she used to sleep standing up."

"Are the muscles above and around her tail becoming flabby?"

"We'll check."

The next day the boys came bursting into the office, quite out of breath. "Midge has kind of pearls on the tips of her teats."

Dr. Winquist clapped his hands. "Midge is ready! She could foal this very night! Go home and clean her stall. Use plenty of fresh, dry straw. Then stay away!"

Who could stay away? Why not take sleeping bags, and just live in the barn? But Mr. Franklin seemed in league with Dr. Winquist. "You kids all have early morning jobs. You need your sleep," he said. "I'll spend the night in the barn. If Midge needs help, I'll call Dr. Winquist."

Mr. Franklin's rule prevailed. By ten o'clock that night of Thursday, the twelfth of September, the house was dark as the night. But no one slept well. Except Mr. Franklin who had had a grueling day at the office. With a sigh of relief he slid down into his sleeping bag which touched a side of Midge's stall. If she rolled or pawed he would hear the rustle of straw or feel the vibrations made by her body.

He felt a strange kind of contentment. He heard the soft footfalls of Pauline stealing almost soundlessly from her lair in the loft; saw her cat eyes gleaming yellow-green in the dark, as with one graceful leap she was on the ledge of Midge's stall, then landing in the straw with barely a thud. Purring noises followed and high whinnies as if one creature with experience were comforting another who had had none.

Mr. Franklin smiled to himself. He settled deeper into his sleeping bag. Directly he slept. At dawn he had a fearful dream. He saw Joey and Justin riding standing on the backs of twin black horses.

They were circling the sky around a mountaintop until they were
lost on the far side, and when they came back into view all that was
left of them was a cloud of smoke, and the cloud – though distant
– made a small bleating sound. With a jerk Mr. Franklin was wide
awake, his hand already gripping the flashlight. He squirmed free

of his sleeping bag, flung open Midge's door and focused his light on a tiny creature wobbling as if caught in a windstorm. Midge was nosing it in puzzlement.

The quiet suddenly exploded. Joey and Justin were shouting, "It's four o'clock! It's morning! We're coming. . . ready or not!" The dogs repeated the news.

The last quarter of the moon had not yet set, but hovered above the weather vane on the barn. The boys broke into a run, their flashlights leading the way. As they reached the barn they saw Midge's door wide open. They stopped a second, then tiptoed in. Mr. Franklin was sprinkling salt on a small wet colt, rubbing timidly, as though afraid to apply pressure. Midge, they noticed, was doing better with her long washcloth of a tongue.

Joey remembered Dr. Winquist's lesson: He took the towel from his father, who willingly let go, and began rubbing the matted coat in firm circular motions, wondering what color it would be when dry.

Justin seemed almost disinterested in the tottering newcomer. He was sweeping his flashlight back and forth in the dark corners muttering: "There's got to be another. There's got to!" He had almost given up when he spied an uneven place in the straw. It could be Pauline he thought, making a nest for herself, but he saw no movement, felt no warmth. Anxiously he raked the straw with his fingers and all at once he was touching an almost lifeless thing. A foal! "Dad. . . Joey! Come quick! I found the other one, but it's cold and not moving."

Mr. Franklin thrust clean towels in each boy's hands. "Rub! Rub! I'll call Doc."

Dr. Winquist arrived a few minutes later, with a stethoscope around his neck and carrying a bagful of instruments. With swift movements he placed his stethoscope over the foal's heart. Scowling, but nodding at the same time — as if the beat was there, but weak or uneven — he removed two gauze pads from his bag, wet them from a bottle and cleaned out the foal's nostrils.

The entire family huddled in the doorway watched the doctor unwrap a cone-shaped mask with a rubber bag attached. He placed it over the filly's muzzle. In a steady, squeezing rhythm he pumped the bag, forcing air through her nostrils, trying to inflate her

lungs. The doctor's head was cocked, listening for a response. His lips parted in sudden triumph at an outward rush of air.

Never breaking the rhythm of his pumping he clipped out his orders. "Peter! Take that white basin from my bag. You've milked cows; now milk the mare out. We've got to get Midge's first protein milk into the filly's stomach.

"John! Justin! Joey! Pile bales of straw, two-deep, around her until she's lying in a tiny box stall all her own."

Like dock workers John and the twins heaved the bales.

Midge meanwhile was so busy mothering her firstborn she was unaware of the miracle taking place.

"What can I do?" This was Mary, not wanting to be left out.

"Mary! You canvas the neighbors for old-fashioned hot water bottles to create an incubator out of the stall."

By now Peter was delivering the basin full of thick golden milk to the doctor. Matter-of-factly he accepted it and took a stomach tube out of his bag.

The twins cringed. They'd seen the tube used at the clinic in deworming, and they remembered the smell of the medicine and the wild-eyed fear of the horses. But the filly didn't struggle while the precious life-saving milk was siphoned into her stomach.

With the first feeding completed, Dr. Winquist stood up and stretched. "My work is done," he said, wiping his instruments as he put them away. "Now, kids, yours is beginning."

The boys were mopping the sweat from their foreheads and necks. "Wow, Doc! What's next?"

"You've got to keep the filly's lungs clear. She has to be turned every two hours, day and night, and carried to Midge every two hours during the first eight hours to nurse. After that every three or four hours."

"How long will the children have to be lifting the foal? Days? Weeks?" Mrs. Franklin asked the question.

"No telling how long. She'll tell us on the day she clambers over the bales and finds her own way."

"But Winquist, what about school?" It was the first word Mr. Franklin had spoken.

"For heaven's sake, Pete, what better schooling for a farmer's kids than a course in animal husbandry?"

Mr. Franklin laughed. "I couldn't agree more heartily," he said, "and there's no need to take a vote from the children."

Five heads shook vigorously.

The doctor snapped his bag shut. "I'll be off, soon as I watch you deliver Teeny to Midge for her first natural feeding."

"*Teeny?*" the children repeated in one voice. "How'd you know her name?"

"I didn't! Well, is it? Don't keep me in suspense!"

Young Peter explained. "Nobody could sleep last night so Mom got the calendar and pointed to the date, Friday the Thirteenth."

"Yeah," Joey chimed in. "'Friday's the big colt, and his twin is 'The Thirteenth.'"

Dr. Winquist bellowed his laughter. "'Teeny' for short of course. Now let's see you operate as a team. Peter, you lift, and Joey or Justin you point Teeny's muzzle toward Mini's bag."

"I know how! I've done this for Pauline." It was Joey doing instead of explaining. He squeezed some of Midge's milk onto his finger tips, and let Teeny suck them, luring her by dribbles closer and closer to Midge until she was suckling noisily.

"How did it feel?" Justin asked Joey when Teeny was back in her incubator.

Joey laughed in pure joy. "She bit my finger!"

"How could she?"

"She has two teeth above and two below."

The morning passed in a kind of radiance. Well-wishers brought enough hot water bottles to convert Teeny's stall into an intensive care unit. School was forgotten. Prayers remembered. "Dear God, thank you for making Friday strong, but please God let The Thirteenth hang in there. Friday'd be missing somebody all his life if Teeny dies; only me and Justin know how it'd be."

The family grew more united than ever. Alarm clocks clanged every two hours. Sleepless children heated kettles of water, lugged them out to the barn, refilling lukewarm bottles.

If Teeny so much as coughed in her sleep prayers were redoubled. When she yawned, happiness flowed from one child to another until such a bond held them that Mrs. Franklin called them "my five-horse hitch, pulling together."

Teeny was learning fast. By afternoon, although she still had to be lifted into place, she found her mother's milk without any coaxing. The twins' only responsibility now was to make sure that she was turned regularly from right side to left, left side to right.

Mr. Franklin joined the night shift beginning at eight. The twin's shift ended then. But this first night they asked to stay behind just a while. Mr. Franklin understood, and returned to the house.

When the boys were alone Joey threw his arms around Midge and kissed her full on the nose. "We'll have wonderful times," he said, "we'll ride into the woods with Teeny and Friday and all the animals tailing along. And we'll help you teach them how to trot and gallop."

"And we'll settle 'em down," Justin added, "when the blacksmith comes to nail on their first shoes."

Midge's ears forked this way and that. She stuck her nose into their hands, as though agreeing precisely. Friday started capering around his mother as if he already knew a thing or two about gaits.

"Joey! Justin! How's our family this evening?"

There in the doorway stood Dr. Winquist, bag in hand.

"Everything's fine!" The twins couldn't hide their surprise at seeing him. "Why are. . . ? Uh. . . what. . . ? Did Dad telephone you to come?"

Without answering Dr. Winquist gave Midge and Friday a friendly move-over smack and went at once to Teeny's incubator. He took his stethoscope from his bag and kneeled down to listen to her heart and lungs. Then he turned to the boys in satisfaction. "Nobody called me to come," he said. "As a boy I used to ride along with my father when he made house calls after hours to visit people who had suffered a crisis during the day. So I decided to make a 'stall call' tonight to see if everything was all right."

"That's great!"

"Doc Winquist, can I ask you a cross-my-heart, hope-to-die question?" This was Justin.

"Fire away, son."

"Did you think Teeny had a chance to live the moment you saw her?" A stillness was broken by Friday bedding down in the straw. Dr. Winquist rubbed his forehead as if to help his thinking.

"Boys," he said at last. "The truth is, I had no time to make a judgment. I said a quick prayer, and felt like. . . "

"Like what?"

"Like I was God's assistant and we cared desperately about that little spark of life."

It was a big answer, and there were no more questions.

Dr. Winquist changed the subject. "You fellows," he said, "might like to know that I'm doing an article for a veterinarian's journal about the rarity of twins in the horse world."

"You are! Will you mention Mini's name. . . ?"

"Of course I will, and Friday's and Teeny's too. When an eleven-year-old mare gives birth to twin foals that live, that's a one chance in 100,000 phenomenon."

"Could we see the magazine when it comes out?" Justin asked.

"You might not want to read it."

"Why?"

"Because I talk of the stigma of twin births."

"What's *stigma* mean?"

"I'm quoting a trainer from Blue Grass Country who out and out said: 'We're not interested in twins. Often one is a weakling and isn't wanted.'"

Justin and Joey looked at each other in disbelief. Midge nosed in, as though this was her concern too.

"When this happens," the doctor continued, "the breeder sometimes forgets there ever was a twin."

"Stigmas stink!" Joey said. "Don't they, Doc?"

Teeny made a whuffing sound in her sleep. The doctor smiled. "If I were writing a storybook instead of a technical article, I would write about a horse breeder who tried to forget when his world-famous mare gave birth to twins; and I'd have him sell off the weaker one, and keep the other one half-hidden to see if it would amount to anything."

"Then what happens?" in unison.

"In *my* book it would turn out that the weaker of the two developed into a champion parade horse, and she would lead the Inaugural Parade for the President of the United States."

"Maybe," Justin announced, with a gleam in his eye. . . "when I grow up *I'll* write that story."

"But Doc," Joey interrupted, "if twins in the horse world are so sickly how can we be sure to raise Teeny?"

"You can't be sure. Nothing is certain. There are no guarantees. But a foal like Teeny that lives sixteen hours after birth and is drinking her mother's milk. . . seems to me that foal's not only going to live, but she'll be quite a contender in the Pet and Pony Show."

A grunt from Teeny's incubator seemed to settle the matter.

"See! She knows she's going to be a winner," Justin exclaimed.

"Yeah," Joey agreed, " a real champ!"